THE LOUD HOUSE

#8 "LIVIN' LA CASA LOUD!"

PAPERCUTZ™
New York

THE LOUD HOUSE

#8 "LIVIN' LA CASA LOUD!"

"LITTLE BIG TOP"
Ronda Pattison — Writer, Artist, Colorist
Wilson Ramos Jr. — Letterer

"HIDE AND SNEAK"
Derek Fridolfs — Writer
Daniela Rodriguez — Artist, Colorist
Wilson Ramos Jr. — Letterer

"FASHION VICTIM"
Hannah Watanabe-Rocco — Writer
Angela Zhang — Artist, Colorist
Wilson Ramos Jr. — Letterer

"FEEDING FRENZY"
Brian Smith — Writer
Isaiah Kim — Artist
Ronda Pattison — Colorist
Wilson Ramos Jr. — Letterer

"SNOWBALL-ED!"
Ronda Pattison — Writer, Artist, Colorist
Wilson Ramos Jr. — Letterer

"SUPER HANGOUT TIME ACTIVATE"
Hannah Watanabe-Rocco — Writer
Chris Sabatino — Artist, Colorist
Wilson Ramos Jr. — Letterer

"STUDY BUDDIES"
Hannah Watanabe-Rocco — Writer
Angela Zhang — Artist, Colorist
Wilson Ramos Jr. — Letterer

"RAIN, RAIN, HERE TO STAY"
Andrew Brooks — Writer
Erin Hyde — Artist, Colorist
Wilson Ramos Jr. — Letterer

"CITY TRICKERS"
Andrew Brooks — Writer
Gizelle Orbino — Artist, Colorist
Wilson Ramos Jr. — Letterer

"PARTY ANIMALS"
Derek Fridolfs — Writer
Chris Sabatino — Artist
Zazo Aguiar — Colorist
Wilson Ramos Jr. — Letterer

"GOSSIP GUY"
Derek Fridolfs — Writer
Melissa Kleynowski — Penciler
Zazo Aguiar — Inker, Colorist
Wilson Ramos Jr. — Letterer

"WASHED UP"
Derek Fridolfs — Writer
Kelsey Wooley — Artist, Colorist
Wilson Ramos Jr. — Letterer

"LIFE IMITATES ART"
Angela Entzminger — Writer
Ivy Jordan — Artist, Colorist
Wilson Ramos Jr. — Letterer

"THE GREAT ESCAPE"
Derek Fridolfs — Writer
Suzannah Rowntree — Penciler
Zazo Aguiar — Inker, Colorist
Wilson Ramos Jr. — Letterer

"THE MASKED MAN"
Derek Fridolfs — Writer
Ivy Jordan — Artist, Colorist
Wilson Ramos Jr. — Letterer

"MY BOBBY AND ME"
Angela Entzminger — Writer
Way Singleton — Artist, Colorist
Wilson Ramos Jr. — Letterer

MIGUEL PUGA — Cover Artist
JORDAN ROSATO — Endpapers
JAMES SALERNO — Sr. Art Director/Nickelodeon
JAYJAY JACKSON — Design
PRINCESS BIZARES, CARLO PADILLA, SEAN GANTKA, ANGELA ENTZMINGER, DANA CLUVERIUS, MOLLIE FREILICH — Special Thanks
JEFF WHITMAN — Editor
IZZY BOYCE-BLANCHARD — Editorial Intern
JOAN HILTY — Editor/Nickelodeon
JIM SALICRUP
EDITOR-IN-CHIEF

ISBN: 978-1-5458-0343-1 paperback edition
ISBN: 978-1-5458-0342-4 hardcover edition

Papercutz books may be purchased for business or promotional use. For information on bulk purchases please contact Macmillan Corporate and Premium Sales Department at (800) 221-7945 x5442.

Printed in China
November 2019

Distributed by Macmillan
First Printing

MEET THE LOUD FAMILY *and friends!*

LINCOLN LOUD
THE MIDDLE CHILD (11)

At 11 years old, Lincoln is the middle child, with five older sisters and five younger sisters. He has learned that surviving the Loud household means staying a step ahead. He's the man with a plan, always coming up with a way to get what he wants or deal with a problem, even if things inevitably go wrong. Being the only boy comes with some perks. Lincoln gets his own room – even if it's just a converted linen closet. On the other hand, being the only boy also means he sometimes gets a little too much attention from his sisters. They mother him, tease him, and use him as the occasional lab rat or fashion show participant. Lincoln's sisters may drive him crazy, but he loves them and is always willing to help out if they need him.

LORI LOUD
THE OLDEST (17)

As the first-born child of the Loud Clan, Lori sees herself as the boss of all her siblings. She feels she's paved the way for them and deserves extra respect. Her signature traits are rolling her eyes, texting her boyfriend, Bobby, and literally saying "literally" all the time. Because she's the oldest and most experienced sibling, Lori can be a great ally, so it pays to stay on her good side, especially since she can drive.

LENI LOUD
THE FASHIONISTA (16)

Leni spends most of her time designing outfits and accessorizing. She always falls for Luan's pranks, and sometimes walks into walls when she's talking (she's not great at doing two things at once). Leni might be flighty, but she's the sweetest of the Loud siblings and truly has a heart of gold (even though she's pretty sure it's a heart of blood).

LUNA LOUD
THE ROCK STAR (15)

Luna is loud, boisterous and freewheeling, and her energy is always cranked to 11. She thinks about music so much that she even talks in song lyrics. On the off-chance she doesn't have her guitar with her, everything can and will be turned into a musical instrument. You can always count on Luna to help out, and she'll do most anything you ask, as long as you're okay with her supplying a rocking guitar accompaniment.

LYNN LOUD
THE ATHLETE (13)

Lynn is athletic and full of energy and is always looking for a teammate. With her, it's all sports all the time. She'll turn anything into a sport. Putting away eggs? Jump shot! Score! Cleaning up the eggs? Slap shot! Score! Lynn is very competitive, but despite her competitive nature, she always tries to just have a good time.

MR. COCONUTS

Luan Loud's wise-cracking dummy.

LUAN LOUD
THE JOKESTER (14)

Luan's a standup comedienne who provides a nonstop barrage of silly puns. She's big on prop comedy too – squirting flowers and whoopee cushions – so you have to be on your toes whenever she's around. She loves to pull pranks and is a really good ventriloquist – she is often found doing bits with her dummy, Mr. Coconuts. Luan never lets anything get her down; to her, laughter IS the best medicine.

EL DIABLO

LOLA LOUD
THE BEAUTY QUEEN (6)

Lola could not be more different from her twin sister, Lana. She's a pageant powerhouse whose interests include glitter, photo shoots, and her own beautiful, beautiful face. But don't let her cute, gap-toothed smile fool you; underneath all the sugar and spice lurks a Machiavellian mastermind. Whatever Lola wants, Lola gets – or else. She's the eyes and ears of the household and never resists an opportunity to tattle on troublemakers. But if you stay on Lola's good side, you've got yourself a fierce ally – and a lifetime supply of free makeovers.

LUCY LOUD
THE EMO (8)

You can always count on Lucy to give the morbid point of view in any given situation. She is obsessed with all things spooky and dark – funerals, vampires, séances, and the like. She wears mostly black and writes moody poetry. She's usually quiet and keeps to herself. Lucy has a way of mysteriously appearing out of nowhere, and try as they might, her siblings never get used to this.

LANA LOUD
THE TOMBOY (6)

Lana is the rough-and-tumble sparkplug counterpart to her twin sister, Lola. She's all about reptiles, mud pies, and muffler repair. She's the resident Ms. Fix-it and is always ready to lend a hand – the dirtier the job, the better. Need your toilet unclogged? Snake fed? Back-zit popped? Lana's your gal. All she asks in return is a little A-B-C gum, or a handful of kibble (she often sneaks it from the dog bowl).

FANGS

WALT

HOPS

CLIFF

LISA LOUD
THE GENIUS (4)

Lisa is smarter than the rest of her siblings combined. She'll most likely be a rocket scientist, or a brain surgeon, or an evil genius who takes over the world. Lisa spends most of her time working in her lab (the family has gotten used to the explosions), and says her research leaves little time for frivolous human pursuits like "playing" or "getting haircuts." That said, she's always there to help with a homework question, or to explain why the sky is blue, or to point out the structural flaws in someone's pillow fort. Lisa says it's the least she can do for her favorite test subjects, er, siblings.

LILY LOUD
THE BABY (15 MONTHS)

Lily is a giggly, drooly, diaper-ditching free spirit, affectionately known as "the poop machine." You can't keep a nappy on this kid – she's like a teething Houdini. But even when Lily's running wild, dropping rancid diaper bombs, or drooling all over the remote, she always brings a smile to everyone's face (and a clothespin to their nose). Lily is everyone's favorite little buddy, and the whole family loves her unconditionally.

CHARLES

BITEY

GEO

RITA LOUD

Mother to the eleven Loud kids, Mom (Rita Loud) wears many different hats. She's a chauffeur, homework-checker and barf-cleaner-upper all rolled into one. She's always there for her kids and ready to jump into action during a crisis, whether it's a fight between the twins or Leni's missing shoe. When she's not chasing the kids around or at her day job as a dental hygienist, Mom pursues her passion: writing. She also loves taking on house projects and is very handy with tools (guess that's where Lana gets it from). Between writing, working and being a mom, her days are always hectic but she wouldn't have it any other way.

LYNN LOUD SR.

Dad (Lynn Loud Sr.) is a fun-loving, upbeat aspiring chef. A kid-at-heart, he's not above taking part in the kids' zany schemes. In addition to cooking, Dad loves his van, playing the cowbell and making puns. Before meeting Mom, Dad spent a semester in England and has been obsessed with British culture ever since – and sometimes "accidentally" slips into a British accent. When Dad's not wrangling the kids, he's pursuing his dream of opening his own restaurant where he hopes to make his "Lynn-sagnas" world-famous.

RONNIE ANNE SANTIAGO

Ronnie Anne's an independent spirit who's into skating, gaming and pranking. Strong-willed and a little gruff, she isn't into excessive displays of emotion. But don't be fooled – she has a sweet side, too, fostered by years of taking care of her mother and brother. And though her new extended family can be a little overwhelming, she appreciates how loving, caring, and fun they can be.

BOBBY SANTIAGO

Ronnie Anne's older brother, Bobby is a sweet, responsible, loyal high-school senior who works in the family's bodega. Bobby is very devoted to his family. He's Grandpa's right hand man and can't wait to one day take over the bodega for him. Bobby's a big kid and a bit of a klutz, which sometimes gets him into pickles, like locking himself in the freezer case. But he makes up for any work mishaps with his great customer skills – everyone in the neighborhood loves him.

MARIA CASAGRANDE SANTIAGO

She's the mother of Bobby and Ronnie Anne. A hardworking nurse, she doesn't get to spend a lot of time with her kids, but when she does she treasures it. Maria is calm and rational but often worries about whether she's doing enough for her kids. Maria, Bobby, and Ronnie Anne are a close-knit trio who were used to having only each other – until they moved in with their extended family.

HECTOR CASAGRANDE

He's the father of Carlos and Maria and the grandfather of six. The patriarch of the Casagrande Family, Hector wears the pants in the family (or at least thinks he does). He is the owner of the bodega on the ground floor of their apartment building and takes great pride in his work, his family, and being the unofficial "mayor" of the block. He's charismatic, friendly, and also a huge gossip (although he tries to deny it).

ROSA CASAGRANDE

She's the mother of Carlos and Maria and wife to Hector. Rosa is a gifted cook and has a sixth sense about knowing when anyone in her house is hungry. The wisest of the bunch, Rosa is really the head of the household but lets Hector think he is. She's spiritual and often tries to fix problems or illnesses with home remedies or potions. She's protective of all her family and at times can be a bit smothering.

CARLOS CASAGRANDE

He's the father of four kids (Carlota, CJ, Carl, and Carlitos), husband of Frida, and brother of Maria. He's a professor of marine biology at a local college and always has his head in a book. He's a pretty easygoing guy compared to his sometimes overly emotional relatives. Carlos is pragmatic, a caring father, and loves to rattle off useless tidbits of information.

FRIDA PUGA CASAGRANDE

She's the mother to Carlota, CJ, Carl, and Carlitos and wife to Carlos. She's an artist-type, always taking photos of the family. She tends to cry when she's overcome with sadness, anger, happiness… basically, she cries a lot. She's excitable, game for fun, passionate, and loves her family more than anything. All she ever wants is for her entire family to be in the same room. But when that happens, all she can do is cry and take photos.

CARLOTA CASAGRANDE

The oldest child of Carlos and Frida. She's social, fun-loving, and desperately wants to be the big sister to Ronnie Anne. Carlota has a very distinctive vintage style, which she tries to share with Ronnie Anne, who couldn't be less interested.

CJ (CARLOS JR.) CASAGRANDE

CJ was born with Down syndrome. He's the sunshine in everyone's life and always wants to play. He will often lighten the mood of a tense situation with his honest remarks. He adores Bobby and always wants to be around him (which is A-OK with Bobby, who sees CJ as a little brother). CJ asks to wear a bowtie every day no matter the occasion and is hardly ever without a smile on his face. He's definitely a glass-half-full kind of guy.

CARL CASAGRANDE

Carl is 6 going on 30. He thinks of himself as a suave, romantic ladies' man. He's confident and outgoing. When he sees something he likes, he goes for it (even if it's Bobby's girlfriend, Lori). He cares about his appearance even more than Carlota and often uses her hair products (much to her chagrin). He hates to be reminded that he's only six and is emasculated whenever someone notices him snuggling his blankie or sucking his thumb. Carl is convinced that Bobby is his biggest rival and is always trying to beat Bobby (which Bobby is unaware of).

CARLITOS CASAGRANDE

The redheaded toddler who is always mimicking everyone's behavior, even the dog's. He's playful, rambunctious, and loves to play with the family pets.

| LALO | SERGIO |

LIFE WITH THE LOUDS

15

"HIDE AND SNEAK"

"FASHION VICTIM"

21

"SNOWBALL-ED"

"STUDY BUDDIES"

"RAIN, RAIN, HERE TO STAY"

"CITY TRICKERS"

WE'RE OFF TO *GREAT LAKES CITY*. *LORI* HAS A DATE WITH BOBBY...

...WHICH MEANS I GET TO TAG ALONG AND HANG OUT WITH *RONNIE ANNE* TODAY.

BABE!

BOO BOO BEAR!

'SUP, LAME-O?

SAVED ME A CHIP?

"GOSSIP GUY"

49

"THE GREAT ESCAPE"

60

WATCH OUT FOR PAPERCUTZ™

Welcome to the entertaining eighth THE LOUD HOUSE graphic novel, "Livin' La Casa Loud," from Papercutz — those comics-loving gringos dedicated to publishing great graphic novels for all ages. *Hola!* I'm Jim Salicrup, Editor-in-Chief and Erstwhile Bronx *Mercado* Frequenter, and I'm here to offer up a few recommendations for other graphic novel series you may also enjoy… But first, I want to thank you for picking up THE LOUD HOUSE #8. Whether you got this graphic novel either digitally or in print, as a gift, bought it yourself, or borrowed it from a friend or library, we thank you. Why? Because your support makes it possible for us to create even more graphic novels featuring THE LOUD HOUSE. Just like THE LOUD HOUSE has grown to be a super success on Nickelodeon, THE LOUD HOUSE graphic novels are becoming more and more popular every day thanks to fans like you.

We realize you're probably busy, between watching THE LOUD HOUSE on Nickelodeon and collecting the graphic novels, not to mention all the other stuff you're doing… but if you're really enjoying THE LOUD HOUSE graphic novels, and wondering if there might be other Papercutz graphic novels you might enjoy too, well, you're in luck, as I'm happy to mention a few!

©2019 Kadokawa Gempak Starz.

DINOSAUR EXPLORERS — Imagine being flung back in time to the days when dinosaurs walked the earth. Well, that's exactly what happened to Sean, Stone, Rain, and Emily. They, along with scientists Dr. Da Vinci and Diana, are now jumping back through time to the present, but at only so many centuries at a time. As a result, they're able to explore and encounter creatures no man has ever seen alive and in their natural habitat. That may be great for scientific research, but not so good if the dinosaurs happen to be really hungry…

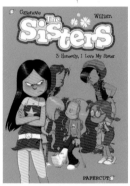

© 2019 BAMBOO ÉDITION.

THE SISTERS — Wendy and her younger sister Maureen love each other, but that doesn't mean they get along perfectly. They're always doing something that will in some way, somehow upset each other. It might be Maureen stealing peeks into Wendy's private diary, or simply misunderstanding what her sister tells her. It's not all bad — Wendy and Maureen also imagine themselves as superheroes fighting side-by-side. No matter what, stuff happens. And it's usually very funny.

©2019 by Geeky Fab Five, Inc.

THE GEEKY F@B 5 — Animal lover Lucy, and her aspiring astronaut sister Marina, have moved to the town of Normal, Illinois, where they have joined three friends from school — math whiz and singer Zara, robotics engineer A.J., and computer coder and fashionista Sofia — to form The Geeky F@b 5. Oh, and their unofficial mascot, Hubble the snarky cat, usually helps out or complicates matters, depending on his unique point of view. Together the girls are able to combine their talents to solve all sorts of problems, because when girls stick together, anything is possible.

While we hope you check out these Papercutz graphic novels, we're sure you won't want to miss THE LOUD HOUSE #9 "Ultimate Hangout" — coming soon! Find out what happens when Lincoln and his friends have the run of the house when his sisters are away for the day…

Gracias,

Jim

STAY IN TOUCH!

EMAIL:	salicrup@papercutz.com
WEB:	papercutz.com
TWITTER:	@papercutzgn
INSTAGRAM:	@papercutzgn
FACEBOOK:	PAPERCUTZGRAPHICNOVELS
FANMAIL:	Papercutz, 160 Broadway, Suite 700, East Wing, New York, NY 10038